Learning to Read, Step by Step!

Ready to Read   Preschool–Kindergarten
• big type and easy words • rhyme and rhythm • picture clues
For children who know the alphabet and are eager to
begin reading.

Reading with Help   Preschool–Grade 1
• basic vocabulary • short sentences • simple stories
For children who recognize familiar words and sound out
new words with help.

Reading on Your Own   Grades 1–3
• engaging characters • easy-to-follow plots • popular topics
For children who are ready to read on their own.

Reading Paragraphs   Grades 2–3
• challenging vocabulary • short paragraphs • exciting stories
For newly independent readers who read simple sentences
with confidence.

Ready for Chapters   Grades 2–4
• chapters • longer paragraphs • full-color art
For children who want to take the plunge into chapter books
but still like colorful pictures.

STEP INTO READING® is designed to give every child a successful
reading experience. The grade levels are only guides. Children can progress
through the steps at their own speed, developing confidence in their
reading, no matter what their grade.

Remember, a lifetime love of reading starts with a single step!

Text copyright © 2002 by Kathryn Heling and Deborah Hembrook.
Illustrations copyright © 2002 by Patrick Joseph.
All rights reserved under International and Pan-American Copyright Conventions.
Published in the United States by Random House Children's Books, a division of
Random House, Inc., New York, and simultaneously in Canada by Random House of
Canada Limited, Toronto.

www.stepintoreading.com

Educators and librarians, for a variety of teaching tools, visit us at
www.randomhouse.com/teachers

Library of Congress Cataloging-in-Publication Data
Heling, Kathryn.
Mouse makes words : a phonics reader / by Kathryn Heling and Deborah Hembrook ;
illustrated by Patrick Joseph.
    p.   cm. — (Step into reading. A step 1 book)
SUMMARY: By dropping the first letter of a variety of words and adding a new letter, Mouse
makes several rhyming words.
ISBN 0-375-81399-3 (trade) — ISBN 0-375-91399-8 (lib. bdg.)
[1. Vocabulary—Fiction.   2. Mice—Fiction.   3. Stories in rhyme.]
I. Hembrook, Deborah.   II. Joseph, Patrick, ill.   III. Title.
IV. Series: Step into reading. Step 1 book.
PZ8.3.H41347   Mo   2003   [E]—dc21   2002013344

Printed in the United States of America   30 29 28 27 26 25 24 23

STEP INTO READING, RANDOM HOUSE, and the Random House colophon are registered trademarks
of Random House, Inc.

MOUSE MAKES WORDS

A Phonics Reader

by Kathryn Heling and
Deborah Hembrook
illustrated by Patrick Joseph

Random House 🏠 New York

Mouse is busy,

Mouse is fast—

grabbing letters

as he runs past.

He finds new ways

to make a rhyme

by switching letters
every time.

Find the word HAT.

Off goes the H.

HAT

Cart in the C.

CAT

Yikes! Now it is CAT!

Find the word FAN.

Blow away the F.

Move in a V.

Honk! Now it is VAN!

Find the word NET.

Scoop up the N.

Push in a P.

Awk! Now it is PET!

Find the word TEN.

Take away the T.

Haul in an H.

Cluck! Now it is HEN!

Find the word WIG.

Wheel away the W.

Along comes a P.

Oink! Now it is PIG!

Find the word PIN.

Pop goes the P.

Carry in a W.

Wow! Now it is WIN!

Find the word MOP.

Wash away the M.

Spin in a T.

Whee! Now it is TOP!

Find the word POT.

Dig up the P.

Roll in a C.

Good night!
Now it is COT!

Find the word CUP.

Wave good-bye to C.

In runs a P.

Arf! Now it is PUP!

Find the word BUG.

Shoo away the B.

Here comes an H.

Hurray!

Now it is HUG!

Mouse is tired.

His work is done.

But moving letters

is so much fun!

Can you keep playing

this rhyming game?

Make more words

that end the same!